Jon Fosse was born in 1959 on the west coast of Norway. Since his 1983 fiction debut, *Raudt, svart* [Red, Black], Fosse has written prose, poetry, essays, short stories, children's books and over forty plays. In 2023, he was awarded the Nobel Prize in Literature 'for his innovative plays and prose which give voice to the unsayable'.

Damion Searls is a translator from German, Norwegian, French and Dutch, and a writer in English. He has translated nine books by Jon Fosse, including the three books of *Septology*.

T0326127

'It ties *2666* by Roberto Bolaño as my favourite book from the twenty-first century... What I read was nothing less than a desperate prayer made radiant by sudden spikes of ecstatic beauty.'
— Lauren Groff, *Literary Hub*

'With *Septology*, Fosse has found a new approach to writing fiction, different from what he has written before and – it is strange to say, as the novel enters its fifth century – different from what has been written before. *Septology* feels new.'
— Wyatt Mason, *Harper's*

'Fosse intuitively — and with great artistry — conveys ... a sense of wonder at the unfathomable miracle of life, even in its bleakest and loneliest moments.'
— Bryan Karetnyk, *Financial Times*

'*Septology* is the only novel I have read that has made me believe in the reality of the divine, as the fourteenth-century theologian Meister Eckhart, whom Fosse has read intently, describes it: "It is in darkness that one finds the light, so when we are in sorrow, then this light is nearest of all to us." None of the comparisons to other writers seem right. Bernhard? Too aggressive. Beckett? Too controlling. Ibsen? "He is the most destructive writer I know," Fosse claims. "I feel that there's a kind of – I don't know if it's a good English word – but a kind of reconciliation in my writing. Or, to use the Catholic or Christian word, peace."'
— Merve Emre, *New Yorker*

'The *Septology* series is among the highlights of my reading life.'
— Rónán Hession, *Irish Times*

Fitzcarraldo Editions
8-12 Creekside
London, SE8 3DX
Great Britain

Copyright © Jon Fosse, 2023
Kvitleik first published in 2023 by Det Norske Samlaget
Translation copyright © Damion Searls, 2023
Published by agreement with Winje Agency AS, Norway

This second paperback edition published in Great Britain
by Fitzcarraldo Editions in 2024

The right of Jon Fosse to be identified as the
author of this work has been asserted in accordance with
Section 77 of the Copyright, Designs and Patents Act 1988.

ISBN 978-1-80427-103-2

Design by Ray O'Meara
Typeset in Fitzcarraldo
Printed and bound by CPI Group (UK) Ltd

fitzcarraldoeditions.com

A Shining
Jon Fosse
tr. Damion Searls

I was taking a drive. It was nice. It felt good to be moving. I didn't know where I was going, I was just driving. Boredom had taken hold of me – usually I was never bored but now I had fallen prey to it. I couldn't think of anything I wanted to do. So I just did something. I got in my car and drove and when I got somewhere I could turn right or left I turned right, and at the next place I could turn right or left I turned left, and so on. I kept driving like that. Eventually I'd driven a long way up a forest road where the ruts gradually got so deep that I felt like the car was getting stuck. I just kept driving, until the car got totally stuck. I tried to reverse but I couldn't, so I stopped the car. Turned the engine off. I was sitting in the car. Yes, well, now I'm here, I thought, now I'm sitting here, and I felt empty, as if the boredom had turned into emptiness. Or maybe into a kind of anxiety, because I felt something like fear as I sat there empty, looking straight ahead as if into a void. Into nothingness. What am I talking about, I thought. There's the forest in front of me, it's just a forest, I thought. All right then, this sudden urge to drive off somewhere had brought me to a forest. And there was another way of talking, according to which something, something or another, led, whatever that might mean, to something else, yes, something else. I peered into the forest in front of me. Forest. Yes. Trees right next to one another, pines, pine trees. And between the trees was brown soil that looked like it was mostly dry. I felt empty. And then this anxiety. What was I scared of. Why was I scared. Was I so scared that I couldn't get out of the car, didn't dare to. Well, this was the end of the forest road I had driven onto and gotten stuck on, I was near where the road ended. And that was probably why I felt this anxiety, because I had gotten my car stuck at the end of a forest road, and here, at the end of the forest road, there was

7

nowhere I could turn around. And I couldn't remember having driven past a shoulder or turn-off since I'd started on this forest road. And that might well be true. Yes, because if I'd seen somewhere to turn around I would definitely have stopped the car and turned around, since it's not like driving on a narrow road through this landscape of low hills was making me feel any less bored, on the contrary, it made the boredom worse. But I hadn't seen anywhere to turn around, I was probably waiting the whole time for one to turn up, yes, waiting to see somewhere I could steer the car to the side, back up a little, drive forward again, maybe do it a few more times, yes, until eventually of course the car would be turned around and I could drive back down the forest road to the main road, and then drive to a town, but what town, to some town anyway, where there were people, and I could maybe buy something, a hot sausage in a bun for example, or maybe, I mean it could happen, I would come across a little roadside coffee shop where I could stop and get myself some dinner. I mean it's possible. And then I suddenly realized it had been several days, I couldn't remember how many, since I'd last had dinner. But that's probably how it is for all of us who live alone. It's like a chore to make yourself dinner, yes, it's just easier to grab whatever's closest, a slice of bread if I have any bread in the house, and put something on it, often it's just mayonnaise on the bread and then two or three slices of lamb sausage. But is that what I should be sitting here thinking about, as if I have nothing more important to worry about. But then what should I be thinking about. But how stupid is that, asking that, thinking that. I went and got my car stuck on a forest road, far away from any people, and I can't get it free, so that means I have more than enough to keep me busy, yes, busy is what they call it, busy getting

8

the car unstuck. Because the car can't just stay stuck how it is now. That's obvious. So obvious that it's just stupid to think like this. I stand there looking at the car, and the car just sits there and kind of looks stupidly back at me. Or maybe it's me looking stupidly at it. And God, how stupid it looks, sitting there stuck on a mound, yes, you'd have to call it a mound, between two ruts right in the middle of the forest road, and the road continues for ten or fifteen more feet until it ends at a footpath leading straight into the forest. And what was I doing on this forest road. Why did I drive into the forest on it. What kind of idea was that. What was my reason for doing it. None. No reason at all. And so why did I drive onto the forest road then. It was purely by accident, maybe. Pure chance. Yes, you probably couldn't call it anything else. But chance, what's that anyway. No, I can't start in with that kind of silly thinking. It never goes anywhere. And what I have to do now is get my car free, yes, just that. And then I have to try to turn it around. But that. Yes, it's because I didn't pass anywhere I could turn the car around, if I had then of course I would've turned around, a long time ago, because this forest road is pretty much the most boring road to drive on that you can imagine. Gentle rolling hills, and other than them the only thing to see was a farm, one abandoned small farm, yes, it must have been abandoned since several windows in the farmhouse had boards of one kind or another nailed over them. And the farmhouse paint was bad, totally gone in many places. And half the roof of the hay barn had collapsed. Rundown houses are sad. Neglected houses. Houses no one cares about. And why doesn't anyone care about them. Because before this house started falling apart it must have been, well, a beautiful house, yes. I would have liked living in a house like that, yes, so I would have liked living in that house, the one I drove past, but it would have had to have been earlier in my life, when I was young, not now. And of course I wouldn't have wanted to live in a house as rundown as that one was now. Now no one could live in it, of course not, not people and not, not what. Animals? Maybe. Yes, maybe animals of some kind had moved in. And the house was probably full of mice. Maybe rats had started living in the house too. Or, well, it doesn't matter. There weren't any people in the house in any case, that's for sure, and what I needed now was a person, someone with a car, or better yet a tractor that could pull the car free. But there was no one in the farmhouse I'd driven past, that's for sure. And then I'd driven a long way without seeing anything but these hills, until I saw a cabin above this forest road, it looked in good shape, like it was being taken care of well enough, but the curtains were drawn so there were no people in the cabin either, that's for sure. And so, yes, so I'd have to go all the way back down to the main road to find anyone. And now that I think about it, I didn't drive past that many houses on the main road either, it was pretty deserted around here, yes, after the last time I turned left or right or whatever it was. Had I driven past any houses at all during that last long stretch I drove on the main road. Maybe. Maybe not. In any case it was a long stretch, the main road was probably going to end before too long and I would have had to turn around there if I hadn't taken a left and started driving up this forest road. Because were there any houses there, along the main road somewhere, no, not that I noticed, not if I turned right and not if I turned left, but then again I wasn't looking for any houses either. Houses hadn't been on my mind, to tell the truth. Of course that didn't mean I hadn't driven past some house or another. Obviously it didn't mean that. I'd driven past more than one house, most likely. And there must have been people living in the houses I must have driven past. Or at least in some of them. Because if no one lived there, why would there be a main road here. Obviously there must have been houses along the main road I'd driven on just now, or maybe not just now, maybe a while ago, yes, before I saw some kind of forest road, some kind of forest road, yes, and I took the left turn and started driving up it. But it was a long way back down to the main road, it would be a long way to walk, and then how far would I have to walk along the main road before I came to a house, no, well, good point. And then when I finally got to a house, there was no way to know if anyone would be home, and if they were home, well, it was by no means certain they'd have a car, or that the person who did have a car would be at home. But when you live like that you need a car. Or maybe not. In the past, nobody had a car. And probably there was a bus they could take. That certainly might be how it was. And in all likelihood I'd driven past a small farm, where they probably had a tractor, a small tractor, maybe a two-wheel tractor. And a two-wheel tractor could definitely pull my car off this damn mound where it was now totally stuck. It's just that it would be a long way to walk on the forest road down to the main road, and then it would probably, no, definitely be a long way I'd have to walk along the main road before I got to the first house. Maybe I should try one more time to get the car free by hitting the gas, going forwards, then putting it in reverse. Forwards, backwards. Again and again. Forwards, backwards. Yes, I'll try that again. And I stay sitting there, and I look straight ahead, but it's sort of like I'm not actually looking at anything, just sitting there. And after a while I think that it's started snowing, really I must have seen it a long time ago but it took me a while before I thought about it, noticed it, but it had already started snowing, not that much, but soft little snowflakes are falling, or drifting, down and down, and I sit there and try to follow the dance of the snowflakes with my eyes, first one flake, then the next, as long as I can follow one snowflake I do it, in the beginning it wasn't so hard, even though I couldn't follow a snowflake for that long, but gradually as it snowed more it got harder to keep my eye on just one flake, and then I couldn't do it any more, and I stopped trying, and then I just sat and looked straight ahead and I thought that now that it had started snowing it was even harder to get the car free, if it was hard before it was completely impossible now. So there was nothing else to do but go get someone who could pull it free. But in that case I couldn't just stay sitting in the car, I had to go find someone. It was just that I didn't know where I could go to find anyone, the small farm I'd seen was abandoned, and no one was in the cabin I'd seen, and it was a long way back down to the main road. And why had I driven so far. Maybe because I was just driving and not thinking about it, I didn't think about how far I had actually driven. Yes, that's probably why. But now, what now. Yes, well, now the only thing to do was find someone with a tractor, or a car, who could pull my car free. But that's just it. Where was I supposed to go to find that someone. I had to walk back down to the main road, then walk as far as I needed along the main road until I got to a house where there was someone who had either a car or a tractor, and people who lived somewhere as inaccessible as this would certainly have a car. They would if they were on the younger side anyway, older people often didn't have cars, they probably never even got a driver's licence, and there'd still be a bus every now and then, even to such a deserted place, because I'd driven for a long time and it was more and more deserted as I went on, yes, I took a left, and I drove until I could turn right, and then until I could turn left again, that's how I kept going all the way until I got here and couldn't go any further. Yes, that's how it is. And now I mustn't wait any longer, I can't. Now something must be done, because now it's snowing like anything. And I just sit and watch the snow fall and fall, or sink and sink, you might call it. And it's getting a little cold, isn't it. Yes it is. But then I can probably just start the engine, I can't believe I didn't think of that before, since after all the car has a good heater. I start the car and turn the heat on full blast. It makes a loud hum. And it doesn't take long before a little warmth starts blowing at me, an even stream clearly separate from the rest of the air. It's nice to feel the heat. And it probably won't be long now before it's all warm in the car. The snow is completely covering the windscreen now, and I turn on the windscreen wipers. I see that it's stopped snowing and the ground out there is white, and the trees in the forest have also turned white. It's beautiful. The white tree, the white ground. And now it's nice and warm in the car. But I can't stay sitting in the car. I need to find someone. And that was probably a path leading into the forest, and it has to lead somewhere, doesn't it, and there must be people there. So maybe I'll walk a little way into the forest on that path. Because I'm sure I'll find some people then. I guess that's what I have to do. Because as long as there's a path, there must be people too. Definitely, I think. In the forest, and probably not that deep inside the forest, there'll be people. It's just about finding them. That's why I can't just stay sitting here in the car. I have to get out. I have to go into the forest. I have to find someone. It's no use just sitting in the car. I turned the key, took it out of the ignition, and put it in my jacket pocket. All right, here we go, I said, and I got out of the car and stood up, I shut the door, and I thought

I should lock it but then realized right away that I didn't need to do that, because if someone wanted to steal the car let them go right ahead, it's not like they could move it from the spot anyway, any more than I could. Well, good. I took a couple of steps and realized I was walking in snow. A thin layer of snow had stuck. I saw that my shoes were leaving a track of footprints in the snow. I saw that the car was covered with snow. The forest road now also looked completely white, it was hard to see exactly where the path was but it was just barely visible, at least I hoped so. I walked into the forest, along the path, yes, where I was walking probably had to be the path, which was winding its way between the trees. Now I just had to keep walking deeper into the forest until I got to a house where someone lived, someone who could help me get the car free so I could drive back to the main road. But I would probably have to drive the car in reverse all the way back down the forest road, no, wait, how could I think that, I could just turn around at the turn-off up to the cabin I had driven past, if not before, of course, yes. And even if it was a long way to the cabin with the curtains drawn, it wasn't that far, it won't be that hard to go in reverse that far, I'm sure, I thought. Now I just had to find someone. That was the only thought in my head now. Find someone. Find someone as soon as I could. Find someone who could help me, but what was I thinking, because it didn't make any sense to go into the dark woods to find someone. I had probably never done anything much worse than this, first getting my car stuck and then walking into the forest to look for help, really, what could have made me think I'd be able to find help in the forest, in the dark woods, that thought, no, it was totally wrong even to call it a thought, it was more like an impulse, a sudden idea, something like that, something I just came up with.

Nonsense is what it was. Pure foolishness. Stupidity. Pure and utter stupidity. And I've never understood why I do things like this. But probably never in my whole horrible life have I ever done anything like this, and how could I, since I've never walked into a forest in late autumn before, and so late in the day, and it's going to get dark soon, soon I won't even be able to see where I am, and then, well, then I won't find anything anywhere, and I won't be able to find my car again either, no, how stupid can I get, no, this is worse than stupidity, this is, no, I don't even have a word for it. And now I can really almost not see anything, it's already got so dark here between the trees. And then this snow. And then this cold. Because I'm freezing. Yes, I'm really freezing, I feel colder than I can ever remember feeling before. But if I can just get back to my car then I can start it, turn on the heater, and warm up, get some heat into me as they say. Get some heat into me. Here in the middle of the dark forest. And I'm so tired. I need to rest for a minute. But where can I sit down. There, over there, isn't that a stone over there. Yes it is, a big round stone in the middle of the forest, a stone that looks like it was made to sit on, and branches hanging over it, pretty far up the trunk, like a roof. And white snow on the branches. The snow I'm standing on is white, and the snow over there on the branches is white. And so here's a stone, right in front of me, big and round and like it was made to sit on. I have to rest for a minute. I have to sit down on the stone. But can I, really, since I'm so cold. I'm shivering. But I'm so tired. I have to sit down on the stone. I go and sit down on the stone. But I feel just as tired, and I'm shivering just as much. Or maybe now that I'm sitting on the stone I'm even colder than when I was standing and looking at the stone, and much colder than when I was walking among the trees. And so there's probably no point in sitting here on this stone. I can't rest, and it just makes me colder. I have to stand up. I can't stay sitting here on this stone. I stand up. I need to find someone, or else I have to go back to my car and then I can either find someone tomorrow, yes, when it's light, yes, when it might even be sunny. The sun can come out, after all, and the sun can really warm you up at this time of year, yes. So if only I knew where to go to get back to my car, but I don't. I guess I'll have to just walk, in one direction or another, maybe I'll get back onto the path, and then I can probably just follow my own footprints back to the car. Because my footprints must be clearly visible in the snow. Yes, I can do that. I want to do that. I want to try to do that. Because what else can I do. In any case I can't just sit on a stone, that's for sure anyway. But it's so dark now that it'll probably be hard to see the footprints even if I do find the path. I need to stand up and I guess I'll just have to walk in one direction or another, then I'll probably find the path. I don't know which direction to go in, and since I don't know, it doesn't matter which direction I go in. I just have to start walking. I walk. I walk straight ahead. I don't think that there's any way this will turn out all right. I'm going to freeze to death. If a miracle doesn't happen, I'll freeze to death. And maybe that was exactly why I walked into the forest, because I wanted to freeze to death. But I don't want to. I don't want to die. Or is that exactly what I do want. But why do I want to die. That's exactly what I don't want, and that's why I want to find my car again so I can warm up. And now I'm walking, now I'm walking as fast as I can, since that gets a little warmth into me, at least I feel a little warmer than when I was sitting on the stone. I keep walking. And before too long I'll probably get back to my car. Because I have to. I didn't walk that far into the forest. I didn't go far at all. But I don't know how far I

16

went, how long a time I walked for, no. It's not far, and it can't be that long. But it's so dark now. I stop for a minute. I look straight ahead, straight into the black darkness, it's like nothing's visible, only black darkness. I look up, straight up, and I see a black sky without stars. Deep in the dark woods, under the dark sky. I stand still. I listen to the nothing. But that's probably just a figure of speech. And if there's one thing I need to avoid now, it's figures of speech. This darkness scares me. I'm scared, that's all there is to it. But it's a calm fear. A fear without anxiety. But I really am scared. Or is that just a word. No, everything inside me is sort of in motion in a way, no, not in one way but in many ways, it's many movements, each disconnected from the others, confused, flailing, jagged, jerky. Yes, that's how it is. I stand and look straight ahead into the impenetrable darkness. And I see the darkness change, no, not the darkness itself, but something separates from the darkness and comes towards me. Now I see it clearly. Something's coming towards me, and maybe it's a person. Or what. Yes, it probably has to be a person. But it can't be a person. It's just not possible that I'm seeing a person, not here, not now. But what is it then. I see the outline of something, and it looks like a person. Because it can't very well be anything else, can it. I stand totally still. I stand like I don't dare move. Now it's really as dark as it can get and there in front of me I see the outline of something that looks like a person. A shining outline, getting clearer and clearer. Yes, a white outline there in the dark, right in front of me. Is it far away or is it nearby. I can't say for sure. It's impossible, yes, impossible to say whether it's close or far away. But it's there. A white outline. Shining. And I think it's walking towards me. Or coming towards me. Because it's not walking. It's just getting closer and closer somehow. And the outline is entirely white. Now I see it clearly. Yes, I see that it's white. A whiteness. It's so clear in the black darkness. So shining white. A shining whiteness. I stand completely still. I'm trying not to move. Just to stand perfectly still. A shining whiteness. An outline of a person. A person inside a shining whiteness. Yes, maybe like that. And is it coming closer. Or going away. No, it's not going away, it's not doing that at least. The shining whiteness keeps getting closer. The outline of what must be a person keeps getting closer. And now I see that the outline has become more of a solid white shape. Yes, a shape. And this shape is expanding more and more. But then it can't be a person who's walking towards me. No, it's impossible. Not here in the forest, not now, in the dark, at night. It can't possibly be a person. But then what is it. Because it looks like a person. It's shaped like a person. I stand completely still. I try to stand as perfectly still as I can. And my body feels almost stiff. And the presence comes closer and closer and becomes more and more, yes, yes, luminous in its whiteness, shining from within, maybe I can put it that way. I take a deep breath. I close my eyes. I think now I'm deep in the dark woods, and it's cold, and I'm freezing. And I see a shining presence right in front of me coming towards me. And now the presence is so close that I could reach out and touch it if I wanted to. But I don't want to touch the presence, because I'm sure that if I reach out my arms to touch the presence I won't feel anything, the presence will be like just empty air, and yet the presence is standing there now, in front of me, it's less than a couple of feet away, and it's probably a woman, if the presence is a person and has any gender at all. No, it doesn't have a gender. It's not a presence with a gender, because it's neither a man nor a woman. But then what kind of presence is it. Should I try to say something to the presence. But I

18

can't really talk to thin air, thin air, thin air, and, yes, well, to what. I just stood there. I didn't move. I looked at the shining presence, surrounded by darkness, and now it was shining white within the outline I saw first. Everything inside the outline was now a shining whiteness too. The light was bright but it didn't hurt to look at it. It was nice to look at. It was weirdly nice to look at. The white presence and me. Should I say something to it. Or should I go. But the presence was standing right in front of me, and I couldn't walk straight into it. Or maybe I could. Yes, I could walk straight into the presence. But no, I couldn't do that. It would be just wrong to do something like that. I just stood there. But what I was seeing couldn't be real, so that meant I'd started seeing things. But was this a vision and not reality. Wasn't the white presence real. Maybe I could carefully try to touch it to find out. But you can't just touch a whiteness like that. Because if you did you'd probably get it dirty. And imagine getting something so white dirty. No, how could I even think of doing something like that. Or maybe I hadn't thought about doing it, the thought had just sort of popped up, but only as a thought, not as something I was actually thinking about doing. No, of course not. And so I just stood there, in front of the presence in all its whiteness. What else could I do. I just stood there, stiffly. But it was strange, I didn't feel cold any more. I wasn't freezing any more, instead I felt warmth coming at me from the presence. Or maybe it wasn't from the presence. But then why did I feel so much warmer than I'd felt before the presence had come, and didn't I feel warmer and warmer the closer the presence came, yes, that's how it was. Now that I thought about it, that's how it was. The closer the presence had come, the warmer I'd felt. That's how it was, like it or not. No getting around it. But now why was this presence standing there in front of me in all its whiteness. It had suddenly just come walking towards me, there in the darkness, and then it stopped in front of me. At first I saw it just as a white, yes, shining outline, and then as a shining presence. But I couldn't just stay standing here like this in front of this presence shining like that in all its whiteness. You can't do things like that, no, absolutely not. Suddenly I felt something like a hand on my shoulder, heavily but in a way lightly. Or an actual hand. No, it wasn't a hand, but it felt like a hand, and so what was it, since, or maybe if, it wasn't a hand. And then something like an arm, yes, it had to be an arm, was laid over my shoulders and holding me, lightly, but I could feel it. I stand as still as I can, completely motionless, or as motionless as I can be, at least. Because what else should I do, what else could I do. I couldn't turn away from the shining presence and run away, into the thickest darkness. Please. Wouldn't the presence just follow me. Or had I now become something like a part of the shining presence. But how could something like that be possible. For the shining presence's arm, if that's the right thing to call it, now felt something like inseparable from my body, and to find out whether it was or not, to be able to find out, I would have to move, and that's exactly what I had no desire to do, or what it felt like I wasn't allowed to do. And this prohibition was binding and unalterable, that's how it felt. I stayed standing still. I breathed regular, inaudible breaths. Because I didn't want my breaths to bother the presence either, yes, this white presence shining in all its whiteness. And then I felt the shining presence's hand being gently taken off my shoulder. And just then I realized I had my eyes closed, I didn't know how long I'd been standing like that, and now when I opened my eyes I didn't see the white shining presence any more. I looked all around but it was nowhere to be seen. And now I could move, and I turned around and I looked into the black darkness. All I saw was darkness. Same as before. But where had the presence gone. Had it just vanished. Disappeared. Just like that. It came slowly and was suddenly gone. What's happening here in the middle of the forest, in the black darkness of the trees, where there's white snow on the branches and on the ground between the trees. That's what's here. That and me. And then this shining presence, but it's not here any more, or maybe it is but I just can't see it, maybe the presence is gone and I say: are you there – and I get no answer and I think of course the presence isn't answering, because whatever it was it wasn't a person, but, yes, well, it wasn't a ghost either, but maybe, maybe, maybe it was actually an angel, maybe it was an angel of God. Because that presence was so shining, so white, or maybe it was an evil angel. Because evil angels are angels of light too, maybe all angels radiate white, both the good ones and the evil ones. Or maybe all angels are both good and evil, it certainly might be like that too. And I say: are you there – and I hear a voice say: yes, yes, yes I'm here now, why do you ask – and I say: do you know who I am – and the voice asks why am I talking to it and I don't know what to say, because I so firmly believed that it was the presence radiant with whiteness that I was talking to and getting answers from, I was so sure of it that I didn't even think about it, but now I think it must be someone, or something, else. But who can it be, is there anyone else here deep in the dark woods, no, so who can it be. But it may well be that there are people besides me in this forest. How can I be so sure that there's just me in this cold dark forest. No, there's absolutely no way to know that, of course not. The forest is big. It's as big as a whole world of its own. And now I'm in this world. And it's dark, so dark and black that I can't see anything, and it's big, the forest is so big that I can't find a way out of it, and it's so dark and black that I can't see anything, or, yes, look there, up there, the moon has come out, yes, and there it is in the sky, so round, so friendly, and there, yes, there are stars in the sky too, lots of stars, clear bright stars, twinkling stars. Yellow moonlight and white twinkling stars. It's beautiful. There's no better word for it, no, not that I can think of anyway. Beautiful. And not long ago, yes, just now, I couldn't see anything in the sky, of course not, because it was snowing, and when it's snowing you can't see the sky, not the moon, if there is a moon, and not the stars, because it's only in clear weather that you can see the moon and the stars. But why am I thinking things like this, what I'm thinking is just completely obvious and nothing worth thinking about, it's just the way it is. That's just how it is. The moon is shining now, and the stars, purely and simply because it's stopped snowing. That's all it is. Neither more nor less. But what happened to me just now, because didn't I just now see a presence, shining in its own whiteness. Yes, I did. But I couldn't have, apparitions like that don't exist and can't exist, it's unreasonable and impossible. I didn't see an apparition like that. But then what did I see. Was I seeing things, maybe. Maybe I had a vision, as people call it. Yes, all right, I was seeing things. And it's not so strange to see things, trapped as I am in the dark forest, because I can't find a way out of the forest. I've walked in all directions, or so I think, but of course I can't know that for sure, what I can know and do know is that I've walked and walked, and that I've stopped and changed direction several times. And so I must have walked in a lot of different directions, if not all, because obviously I haven't gone in every possible direction since if I had I would have found my car, I would have had to have got back to my car. And if only I'd done that I would now be sitting in my car feeling nice and warm and the snow wouldn't have landed all over me so that I was totally white. Yes, almost as white as that apparition of whiteness I maybe just saw, or maybe saw only as a vision, or like in a vision, maybe that's the best way to put it. But it's nice looking at the stars, and at the moon. Most beautiful of all is the moon, it's so yellow and friendly tonight, I've probably never seen it like this before. And a nice big yellow moon, yes, it, yes, now what was I about to say, it disappeared, it just vanished from me, just like the presence shimmering in whiteness vanished too. Or maybe it's not gone, it's just turned invisible. Maybe I just can't see it now that it's so much brighter. That may well be, so then I can probably ask if it's still here. Wouldn't hurt anyway, and I say: are you there – and I don't hear any answer. And there was probably no reason to expect one, either, but I could always ask again, and I say: is there anybody there – and isn't that a little whisper I hear back saying yes I'm here, yes, well, I guess I do hear it but it's probably just something I'm imagining, because it wasn't a clear voice in any case, and then I hear a voice say: I'm here, I'm here always, I'm always here – which startles me, because this time there was no doubt that I'd heard a voice, and it was a thin and weak voice, and yet it's like the voice had a kind of deep warm fullness in it, yes, it was almost, yes, as if there was something you might call love in the voice. Love, now what do I mean by a word like that, because if there's any word in the world that doesn't mean anything it's that one. But now I'm just talking nonsense, it must be the cold that's making me think like this, and the fear of being trapped in the dark forest. But then again I'm not trapped. It's true that I'm deep in the dark woods but I'm not trapped, I just can't find a way out of the forest and obviously that's different from being trapped or locked in, because in that case there pretty much has to be someone who's locked you in, it can't be the person themself who locks themself in, or maybe it can be the person themself, and if it's me who locked myself in I didn't do it on purpose, I'm trapped totally against my will, in the dark woods, involuntarily self-trapped, if you can put it that way. But that's just words. Words and more words. And now I'm alone, all alone, deep in the dark woods. Or am I alone, no, I can't be, because I was just now talking to someone or something and I say: are you there – and I get no answer, and I say: is anybody there – and I feel something like despair come over me and I say: answer me, can't you answer me, I'm talking to you, and we were talking to each other not that long ago, it was just now – and I turn around and I look all around and I don't see anyone, only trees and more trees, the snow-covered branches there in the moonlight, in the light of the enormous round yellow moon, the endless number of twinkling stars, and then not right under the trees but in some places between the trees there's snow-covered ground, the snow-covered earth that I'm standing on. And it really is so cold, I'm so freezing. I need to get out of the forest before night falls and before I get too tired. Because what's going to happen if I don't get out of the forest. I live alone, after all, so there's no one who'll miss me, and if someone does miss me they still won't know where I am, so no one's going to come looking for me here in the forest, and why would anyone drop by to see me in the first place, to tell the truth I can't remember the last time anyone dropped by to see me, no I won't bother trying to think about that, not now anyway, I have other things to think about now, you can say that again, yes, actually there's really only one thing to think about and that's how I'm going to get out of the forest and find my car again, or find someone who can pull my car free, with a tractor, yes, it'll have to be with a tractor since after all a normal car probably won't want to risk driving up this forest road now that it's snowed as much as it has, no, no one will want to do that, that's obvious, and maybe even someone with a tractor won't want to do it now that it's gotten so dark, because it can be hard to see where the edge of the road is, in the dark now, now that it's snowed, no, even if I find someone who has a tractor there's probably no way I can get the car pulled free tonight, probably no one will be able to help me before morning. But the most important thing now is obviously to get out of the forest and back to some people, people in a warm house, so I can get warm, and, yes, I'm really hungry too, and thirsty, but if only I can find some people I'm sure I can get something to drink and to eat too, and warm up, yes, I'm sure they'll have lit a fire since it's so cold out. It'll be nice and warm in their living room, and the light will be on. The way it should be. Now I just have to start walking so I can find someone. And so now I'm walking, yes, straight ahead, and I have a feeling that someone, or something, is walking next to me, and it must be that presence, mustn't it, the one with its shining whiteness. Yes, it must be. But in any case I don't want to look off to the side, or behind me. Maybe I could ask who it is walking next to me or behind me, but I guess I can't, but why can't I. I mean I can. And I say: who are you – and I don't hear anything, so there's probably no one there, and well why would there be, and I say again: who are you – and a voice says: it's me – and I think that the presence, yes, the presence, because that must be who or what it is, has answered now, so it's probably still walking next to me, or maybe walking behind me. And I say: what do you want from me – and the presence doesn't answer. I say: won't you tell me. And the presence says: I can't tell you. I say: why not – and the presence doesn't answer. I say: can't you say it – and the presence says no. I say: why are you following me. The presence says: I'm not following you. I say: so what are you doing. The presence says: I'm walking with you – and I think that there's no point in asking the presence about anything, but why is it walking with me, in its words. I say: why are you walking with me. The presence says: I can't tell you that. I say: why not. The presence says: because I can't – and I think that asking it questions won't get me anywhere so I might as well just not bother. I say: you can't lead me to any people, can you – and the presence doesn't answer. I say: you can't lead me out of the forest, can you – and the presence doesn't answer, and I think no, well, if it doesn't want to say then it doesn't want to say, but it did answer me a couple of times, so it's there, anyway, there next to me, or behind me, so it's walking with me whether it's next to me or behind me. But who is it. I have no idea, and I probably can't just ask who it is either, but why not. I say: who are you. The presence says: I am who I am – and I think that I've heard that answer before, but I can't remember where I heard it, or maybe I read it somewhere or another. I probably should just stop worrying about the presence, stop thinking about who it is. And now I need to get out of this forest soon, because now I've been here for so long, so infinitely long, at least that's how it feels, and now it's light enough to see anyway, since the moon is so big and yellow, because the moon is suddenly visible again, and before the moon came out it was impossible to see anything, and if only it doesn't get totally dark again now, dark as the blackest night, because if it does I won't know where I'm walking, not that I know it now, but now I can at least see where I'm putting my feet. And there, in front of me. There's something there and it's coming towards me, isn't it. Yes, yes, I believe so, but it's a long way up ahead and it's not so easy to see what it is, because I can just see something darker in the darkness, and it maybe looks like, yes, maybe that's two people walking over here, it could be. But here, now, in the middle of the black dark woods, no, there can't be two people, but what can it be then if it isn't two people, yes, it must be two people. And maybe I can start walking towards them, because nothing could be better than if these are two people, if I could have company, as they say, here in the middle of the forest. But it can't possibly be that there are two more people here who've gotten lost, no, it can't be, and so maybe these are two people who live nearby and who've just gone out for a walk, an evening stroll. But now, when it's dark. In the cold, in the snow. No, impossible. Sensible people don't do that. But then again not everyone is so sensible, I'm not one of the most sensible people myself, someone who walks away from his car into a forest, into the forest, even though it's late autumn and late in the day and even though it was cold I walked away from my car and into the forest. It's unbelievable that anyone would do such a thing. But yes, yes, there really are two people walking towards me, it can't be anything else, and what are they doing in the forest and what am I doing in the forest. I have just as little an idea of what they're doing in the forest as I have of what I'm doing in the forest. And maybe they know just as little about why they're in the forest now as I do. It may well be that they too have lost their way, it's possible. I walk towards them, and it looks to me like they're walking towards me too. And they're walking so close together that they're inseparable, so they must be a couple, and either they're holding hands or one of them

27

is holding the other one's arm. And it looks like they're a couple. And it's probably the man who's a little taller than the woman, but of course it could also be the other way around, she could be taller than him. I walk towards the couple, and the couple walks towards me. It is perfectly clear that not only am I walking towards the couple but that they're walking towards me too. Who could they be. Who in the world could they be. But it was nice to see other people in the forest too, that's for sure. And here they come, walking towards me. Or is it just me who's walking towards them. I think that I'm walking towards them and they're walking towards me. Yes, it must be pretty much like that. But who are they. Who can it be. It's much too dark to see their faces, or clothes, but we're getting closer and closer to each other. And when we get close enough of course I'll be able to see their faces, and their clothes, and then I might know who they are, yes, anyway if I know them, or recognize them, otherwise not, obviously, how can I even think such obvious thoughts. I must really be tired. Or maybe it's the cold that's making me think such idiotic obvious thoughts. I usually never think things like that. I tend to be nice and clear in my thinking. Always. You might almost consider me a thinker. No, now I'm bragging, terribly. And I don't normally do that either, yes, brag, yes, at least when I'm by myself and not alone in a forest, in the forest. And it's probably how cold it is that's making me think not as clearly as I usually do. I can't think of any other reason anyway. But sure enough I'm walking towards two people, and two people are walking towards me. And they look like an elderly couple, an elderly married couple maybe, yes, they must be. Yes, they're an old couple. Now I can clearly see that they must be. But haven't they seen me yet, it doesn't seem like they've seen me anyway. But they must have, maybe I should call out to them, because I could always do that, or maybe that wouldn't be the right thing to do. You shouldn't shout in the forest, at least I've heard people say that. I keep walking towards the old couple, who must probably be a married couple. Yes, they're definitely a married couple. I have to call out to them. I shout: hello there. And I hear: hello. I shout: is anybody there – and I hear a yes and I can hear that it's the voice of an old woman. I hear another yes and now it's the voice of an old man I'm hearing. And then it's silent. Totally silent. Yes, so quiet that it's like you can reach out and touch the silence, and I stop. And then I stand there and listen to the silence. And it's like the silence is speaking to me. But a silence can't speak, can it. Yes, silence can speak in its way, and the voice you hear when it does, yes, whose voice it is. But it's just a voice. There's nothing else you can say about the voice. It's just there. It's there, no doubt about it, even though it isn't saying anything. And then I hear it call out: so, here you are – and I hear that it's the old woman calling that. And the voice says again: here you are. The voice says: finally, we found you – and I think how can it say something like that, because no one's found me. The voice says: now I've found you – and I don't understand anything, whose voice this is, and what it's doing here, deep in the dark woods. I shout: who are you. The voice says: can't you tell from my voice, I'm your mother, can't you tell it's your mother, don't you recognize your own mother's voice, unbelievable, not recognizing your own mother's voice – and I think that this isn't my mother's voice, I know her voice very well and this isn't it, and I have to answer something, I can't just say nothing. I say: it's me. She says: yes, it's you. I say: but what are you doing out here in the forest. The voice says: looking for you. I say: you're looking for me – and the voice says yes and I say why are you doing that. The voice says: because you can't be out in the forest now – and I say no. The voice says: surely you can understand that much – and I say yes. The voice says: it's too cold to be out in the forest now, and it's too dark. I say: yes, you're absolutely right. The voice says: you need to go home. I say: but I can't find my way home. The voice says: you've gotten lost. I say: yes, yes, that's probably true, I have. The voice says: that's why we're coming to help you. I say: thank you, thank you – and now I can clearly see the elderly couple right there in front of me. And yes, yes, that's my mother standing there. No question about it. It can't be anyone else. It's her, my mother. And my father is standing next to her. And he's holding my mother's arm. And it doesn't look like he's really following what's going on. He's just staring straight ahead as if into a void. Into empty space. And I'm probably just staring into empty space too. I certainly am. I stand there. I try to stand totally still. And I see my mother and father coming closer and closer and as the old woman looks at me I hear her say: why are you just standing there, don't just stand there like that, you can't just stand there like that, behave yourself – and I think about what she must mean by that, that I can't just stand here like this and that I have to behave myself. Why can't I stand here like this, and why does standing here like this mean I'm not behaving myself. What am I doing wrong. I can't be doing all that much wrong just standing here without moving. I'm not doing anything. I'm just standing here. What's so wrong about that. It can't be that wrong, can it. And then it shouts again: don't just stand there, you have to do something, you can't just stand there, do something already – and it's my mother shouting and I start walking towards my parents. And my mother says: good, at least you're coming towards us, you're doing that at least, if nothing else – and I think I shouldn't say anything, not because I don't have anything to say but because I don't feel like saying anything, and besides I don't know what I should say, but maybe I can say that I don't understand why they're out in this cold dark forest too, so late in the day, yes, it's night by now, and so late in the autumn, or early winter really, yes, I can probably say that. I say: why are you out in the forest. And she says: that's what you're asking, it's unbelievable that that's what you're asking. I say: why. She says: because you're out in the forest yourself – and I say yes. She says: and what are you doing out in the forest, you're going to freeze to death, you have to go home – and I wonder if I should tell her that I can't find my way out of the forest and ask her if she knows the way out of the forest, but of course she won't know it, because if she did why would she be walking around in the forest and I say: do you know the way out of the forest – and she says: no, but he does – and she looks up at my father and she says: you know the way out of the forest, don't you – and he shakes his head. She says: you don't know the way – and he says no and she says she was sure he knew where the way was, he always knew the way, she couldn't remember a single time when he hadn't known the way, she was sure he knew the way, she would never have imagined anything else, she says and she's stopped, and she's let go of my father's arm and now she's looking up at him, and she says, and her voice sounds scared: you don't know the way, you can't find the way back home – and my father shakes his head. She says: so why did we walk so far into the forest – and my father doesn't answer, he just stands there stiffly. She says: answer me. He says: but we came here together. She says: no, it was you who dragged me into the forest. He says: but you wanted to find him. She says: didn't you

want to find him too. He says: yes, of course – and he
looks down and my mother stands and looks at him, they
stand like that for a long time and neither of them says
anything. She says: yes, well, then we can freeze to death
too, not just him – and he says: we probably might, yes,
it's cold enough, and deep in the cold dark woods where
we've walked, where we've come to. She says: but why
would you bring me so far into the forest when you don't
know the way out. He says: it was you who brought me
into the forest. She says: yes, I guess it was – and it's silent.
Then she says: well, we did it together – and he doesn't
answer and I stand there looking at them. And they look
so old, they look so tired, how can they have aged so much
in such a short time, because it hasn't been that long since
I last saw them, or maybe it has been a long time, maybe
it's been years, or maybe it's been just a few months, or a
few weeks, a few days, because it's definitely been more
than a few hours, that's for certain, yes, I know that much
anyway, but how long it's been exactly, yes, exactly exactly exactly, now there's a word to use in this context, I
could hardly have come up with a less appropriate word,
yes well how long it's been since I last saw them, no, I can't
say, but I'm seeing them now anyway, or can I be sure of
that, maybe I'm just imagining that I'm seeing them, that
might well be, no, it's not like that, they're standing right
there, my mother and father, right there in front of me,
I'm sure of it, and I've talked to them too, or, well, I've
heard them talking to each other. And I think they're
looking for me. Didn't they say that, yes, they said they
were looking for me. I say: are you looking for me – and
there's no answer. I see them standing there, my mother
and father, and they just look at me and they don't answer
when I talk to them, and of course they need to, because
in spite of everything I'm their son and I say: you need to

answer me when I'm talking to you, so answer, don't just stand there, answer me, you need to answer me – and I hear that my voice is begging and pleading, almost pitiful, yes, I'm downright whimpering, you could say, maybe exhausted too, or else it's like it's not my voice, it's like someone else is speaking through me, someone I don't know, a total stranger actually. My mother says: why are you just standing there and I don't say anything – and she looks at my father and she says: say something, why are you just standing there not saying anything, can't you talk, have you lost the use of speech, you need to say something – and my mother looks at my father and she says: say something, you too – and my father doesn't say anything, and she says: it's always the same, you never say anything, not even when your son is standing right in front of you just a few feet away do you say something, can't you say something, you need to say something, you need to say that he has to come with us and then we have to get out of the forest, walk out of the forest together – and my father says yes. My mother says: you can't just say yes – and my father says no, and my mother says: you just say yes or no – and my father says yes and then they just stand there, my mother and father, they stand there stiffly, again they're standing like that and I think that I have to go over to them. It doesn't make any sense to stand at a distance like this and just look at each other. But I stay where I am, and they stay where they are. And so we just stand like that and look at each other and then look down and look back at each other and look back down. No, it can't go on like this, I think. I'll walk over to them now, I think. But I just stay where I am, and I see my mother take my father by the arm and pull a little on his arm, that's what it looks like. But they stay where they're standing. And I stay where I'm standing. And I look up and I see that the stars aren't visible any more, there are clouds covering the stars and everything has gotten much darker. Now the moon is half covered by clouds, I see, and I see clouds moving, covering the whole moon, and then it's totally dark, and I can barely see my mother and father any more. They've disappeared into the darkness, they're both totally covered in darkness now. And I'm alone in the darkness again, exactly like I was before. I can't see anything. And my parents, they were here just now, I saw them, I did. They were here. But where did they go. Well obviously they just disappeared into the darkness, they're not visible now the way nothing is visible when it gets dark enough, black enough. Now the moon is covered by clouds and no one can see anything any more and I hear my mother calling out: where are you – and I hear my father say: here I am – and my mother says she knows that, she's holding his arm, she says, she didn't mean him, she meant me, she says, and my father says: yes, of course, I just answered without thinking – and my mother says: yes, same as always – and it's silent and neither of them says anything. I stand totally silent. I want it to be totally silent, I want to listen to the silence. Because it's in silence that God can be heard. Someone said that, anyway, or something like that, but in any case I can't hear any voice of God, the only thing I can hear is, yes, nothing. When I listen to the nothing, I hear if the nothing can be heard, if that's not just a figure of speech, just something people say, I think, yes, I hear, yes, the nothing, not any thing, not in any case the voice of God, whatever that is. But I'll leave that for other people to decide, I think. And obviously it wasn't my parents I saw just now, that must have been something I just imagined, because I'm alone now, in the dark forest, alone, all alone, as they say, all alone. But haven't I always been like that, all alone, yes, well, I probably have been, maybe, and I hear my mother say: where are you – and it doesn't sound like she's either nearby or far away, it's like it's just her voice that makes a sound, in a way, and then there's silence. She says: where do you think he is – and there's no answer. My mother says: can't you even answer me. My father says: I don't know – and my mother says that of course he doesn't know, he probably doesn't even need to say that, no, if he doesn't have anything else to say besides that he can just keep his mouth shut, she says and my father doesn't answer and my mother says he can at least answer her and my father says that he doesn't know what to say and my mother says that of course he doesn't know that, because no one can know that, as dark as it's gotten now. My father says: no, of course not. And then there's silence again. I stand completely still, completely motionless, and I think that this is probably something I'm just imagining, yes, that my mother and father are in the forest too. I'm in the forest, and I'm totally alone in the forest. There's no one else in the forest, just me. And I probably won't get out of the forest either. And I'm so tired, and it's so cold. But hasn't everything brightened up a bit. I look up and I can see a few stars, I can't see many stars, no, but a few, and now I can also see a bit of the yellow moon again. It's good that there's a little more light, everything's better when I can see a little, yes of course, that goes without saying. But where did my parents go. They were here just now. I didn't just imagine it. I heard them talking. Or it was only my mother talking, same as always, my father just answered her. Everything was the same as before. Yes. But I'm freezing like this. And if only it doesn't start snowing again. But now it's clearing up more and more. I can see better and better. But where did my parents go. They were just standing directly in front of me, even if they were a long way away. But I walked towards them, and they walked towards me, but we were walking so slowly. We walked, we both walked, they did, I did, but it was like we didn't get any closer to each other, actually it was really strange, and impossible to understand, to tell the truth. And where are they now. But it has to be that if I just walk straight ahead we'll probably reach each other, that is, if both, if both they and I, walk straight ahead. And so because of that I should just start walking straight ahead. Then we'll probably end up reaching each other. Or it might happen anyway. Because maybe my parents, my mother and father, are also walking straight ahead. And in that case, we'll walk until we meet up. Since my parents are probably thinking the same thing as me. So then I'll probably just start walking straight ahead then. And now it's so bright that it's possible to walk between the trees, here in the middle of the dark woods. I start walking. And I'm holding both arms ahead of me. And maybe I should call out and ask where they are, where Mother and Father are. But then again I've never called out for Mother and Father, or maybe I did. When I was little anyway. No, I don't believe I did. Mother, Father. No, never. And now they're gone, and maybe they were never even here. Maybe I only imagined they were here. Imagined that I heard my mother talking, that she said something to me. No, that's totally unthinkable. They were here all right. My mother was here. My father was here. I saw them right over there, yes, just there, there, right there. Right over there, yes. Or maybe it was here where I am now that I last saw my parents. Maybe they were standing right here where I am now. That's possible, it may well be that it was here. Yes, I almost think it was here. It was here. Now I'm sure of it. It was here. Nowhere else. Not there, but here. Right here. Not there, but here. Here's where. Maybe I can call out and ask where they are. Yes, that's what I need to do and I call out: where are you – and then I stand there completely quiet and listen, but no one answers, and now that was strange but then I hear my mother say: where are we. Again I hear my mother say: where are we, and now is that something you need to ask, we are where we are, nowhere else, why ask that, why ask where we are – and I say: because, yes, because. And my mother says: we're looking for you. I say: and now you've found me, but where are you. My mother says: we probably just can't see each other since it's so dark – and I say yes and then it's silent and then my mother says I need to go home. I say: I can't find the way, can't you find a way out of the forest either. My mother says: imagine saying something like that, or, what do you think, Father – and my father doesn't say anything, and it's silent for a long time, and then my mother says that my father needs to say something and he says: no we can't find the way – and my mother says that he mustn't say such a thing. My mother says: we'll find the way, we just haven't found it yet, don't you agree – and there's silence. She says: can't you ever answer. My father says: yes, we'll find the way, we certainly will – and again it's silent. My mother says: how do you know – and my father doesn't answer. My mother says: answer me. My father says: I don't know. My mother says: no, no you don't know – and I think that now we're going to find each other soon, meet up with each other, we have to, because it doesn't sound like our voices are that far away from each other, sometimes it sounds like they're right next to each other, and sometimes like they're far away from each other, I think, and it's really so strange that it's like this, that the voices are close to each other at some times and far away at other times. No, I don't understand it. It's impossible to understand. But there are lots of things that are impossible to understand, like for example that I'm deep in the dark forest now, in the dark woods. And then my mother suddenly calls out: where are you – and her voice is both very nearby and very far away at the same time, and it's impossible to understand how a voice can be both very nearby and very far away, and that's why I can't walk towards where the voice is coming from either, I think, and I hear my mother call out: you need to come here now, we need to go back home soon now, Father and I – and I answer that I'm coming as fast as I can, but the thing is I don't know where I'm supposed to go, I say, and my mother says isn't that just like me, I'm always like that, that's how I've always been, she says, I've always just done whatever I wanted, never what she wanted, I've always just listened to myself, and now, yes, now I'll see how that ends, she says, it'll end the way it has to end, the way it had to end, my mother says, and I don't know what to say and I hear my mother say no, this won't work, she's going to freeze to death, she says, and I think why doesn't my father say anything, but then again he never really has, I think. And it's so cold, and I'm so tired. I have to sit down and rest for a bit. But I can't just sit down on the ground between the trees, can I, but there, over there, is a stone, a round stone, right in the middle of the forest too, and now that's strange, because how could that stone have ended up there, no, it's impossible to understand. It couldn't have rolled there, and no one could have brought it there, put it there. Why would they even want to. But anyway, the stone is there now. It's sitting there, and someone can sit on it. I have to sit down on that stone there. And why don't I. Why am I just staying here. I can move as much as I want, right. I can go wherever I want, right. Nobody can tell me not to. No one, no. And so why am I just standing. Why don't I do anything then. Maybe because I'm tired, but isn't that exactly why I want to sit down on that round stone, to rest a bit. Yes, that's what I want to do. Right now, this instant. I go over to the stone and I sit down on it. And since there are branches above the stone there's no snow on it. I'm sitting safe and sound on the stone. And it felt good to sit down. To take a little break. Only now can I feel how truly tired I was. And, yes, how sleepy I am. I'm really tired, and it's no wonder really since I drove a long way and walked in the forest for a long time, walked a long way and for a long time. Far and farther than far. Yes, you could put it that way. And then I hear my mother say wasn't he always his own person, and my father says: yes, yes he was, always – and my mother says: yes, so he was – and I hear my father say yes. And I feel the tiredness that has come over me. But I mustn't fall asleep now. I have to stay awake now. It's important now. It's the most important thing now. Falling asleep in the snow now, no, unthinkable. I can't do that. Because then I'll die. Then I'll freeze to death. But I can rest for a bit anyway. Surely I can do that. Yes, of course. I need to have a little rest since I'm so tired and since I need to find a way out of the forest and in that case I can't be so tired. Rest. Just rest. Not think about anything in particular, but rest. Just rest. Just be there. And look. But look, look over there, yes, over there between two trees, yes, there, yes, yes, there's a man standing there. And he's dressed in a black suit. And he's wearing a white shirt. And a black tie. And he's barefoot. He's standing there barefoot in the snow. But that's not possible. Now I really am seeing things. Now I'm out of my mind, as they say. But he's standing there, he really is, a man in a black suit with a white shirt and a tie, yes, he's standing there and he's definitely looking at me. Yes, he is. Now I see it, without a doubt, he's looking at me. Straight at me. He's not just looking at me, he's looking straight at me. Why is he doing that. Here, here in the middle of the dark woods, there's a man in a black suit looking at me. No, it's not possible. It can't be. It's not possible. And the man is standing there completely motionless. Or is he moving a little. Maybe a little. But in any case just barely. Or maybe he isn't moving. Maybe I'm just imagining he's moving. Could be. But in any case, yes, in any case. In any case what. What. What do I mean by that. In any case what. And my parents, yes, where did they go. And the white presence, the one that shimmered in all its whiteness and that I saw just the shimmering outline of at first, yes, where did that go. But aren't I seeing it over there now, yes, on the other side of the man in the black suit. There, over there. Yes, yes, now I can see the white presence again. It's standing there. And it too is standing completely motionless, and yes, yes, it's still shining, yes, that sort of shimmering light is still coming from the presence. I don't understand this. It's beyond my understanding, as people like to say. Figure of speech, figure of speech. But to speak at all reasonably now, the way things are at the moment, yes, well, that doesn't seem very reasonable, no now I'm about to start laughing, yes, that too. But laughing when things are the way they are now, no, there are limits. But actually it doesn't seem like there are any limits. Everything is sort of beyond the limits, it's like being locked into a closed room in the forest, trapped, but at the same time it's like the room is unbounded. It's not possible. Either it's like this or it's like that. This way or that way, yes. Mother or Father. The white presence or the man in a black suit. Either I stay in the forest or I get out of the forest. Either or. And either my car will just stay stuck or I'll get it unstuck. That's how it is. Either or. But it was really nice to sit down. I really needed to rest. Only now do I realize how tired I am. I was much tireder than I

40

thought. I was really about to fall asleep here, sitting on this round stone, under the branches with all the snow on them. I'm sitting on the round stone with the branches as a kind of roof. It's almost like a little house I've made for myself. House. No, how can I think that. If there's one thing in the world that's not like being in a house then it's probably this, sitting where I'm sitting now, here outside, under the open sky, with only a few branches over my head, and sitting on a round stone too, a stone that seems like it was made to sit on, sitting on a stone under branches with snow on them deep in a forest, deep in the forest. I'm tired and I want to lie down. But I can't do that, because then I might fall asleep and I can't do that, not here in the dark forest. Deep in the dark woods. I close my eyes. But even when I close my eyes I only see thick darkness. Nothing else, just black, just dark. And then that man I saw in a black suit. And with a white shirt and a black tie. And wasn't he barefoot too. Yes, barefoot in the snow. Wasn't he. Yes, I believe he was. Yes, he was barefoot, I saw it, but in a way it was also like I didn't see it. That's how it must have been. I open my eyes. And now the man in a black suit is standing almost right in front of me. He's standing there looking straight at me. Who can he be. And now I see clearly that he's barefoot. He's standing barefoot in the white snow. Like he can do that. But anything's possible. Everything. All together. Anything can happen. Standing barefoot in the snow too, in the middle of the forest, deep in the dark woods, dressed in a black suit, white shirt, and black tie. That can happen too. Even that. And there, not too far from the man in the black suit, yes, if it isn't the radiant presence, yes, the presence shining in its whiteness. And now the whole presence is shining. No, I don't understand this. It's not something that can be understood either, it's something

41

else, maybe it's something that's only experienced, that's not actually happening. But is it possible to only experience something and not have it be happening. Everything you experience, yes, is real in a way, yes, and you probably understand it too, in a way. But it doesn't matter either way. Because there it is, the presence, it shines shimmering in its whiteness, and there's the man in the black suit, barefoot in the snow, there, behind the shimmering presence, a little off to one side of him, and there, behind the man in the black suit, between him and the shimmering presence, there, yes, there are my parents, my mother and father, now they're standing there holding hands. Their arms are hanging down between the two of them like a V. Yes, it's them. It's my parents. And they're looking at me. Straight at me. And now I see the man in the black suit turn towards them, towards my parents, but they sort of don't notice him, they seem to just be looking at me. But they don't say anything. Maybe I should say something to them. But what should I say. I don't know what to say. I never have, but still, something needs to be said, or maybe nothing needs to be said just now. That may well be. In any case I don't say anything, and I'm not planning to say anything either. I'm just sitting here. I'm sitting here on the round stone and now I see that the man in the black suit has started walking towards my parents. He walks slowly, step by step, towards them, barefoot in the snow. And now I won't say anything and I don't want to either. I look at the man in the black suit, I see him slowly get closer to my parents, my mother and father, and it's like they don't notice him, they're just looking at me. Can't they stop looking at me now. Why do they keep looking at me. Just at me, not at anything else. Can't they look at something else now. At the man in the black suit maybe. Yes, why don't they look at him, since after all he's walking towards them. Don't they see that he's walking towards them. It's like he's invisible to them, yes, it's like they don't see him. Or do they sort of want me to think that they can't see him. Maybe that's how it is, and maybe it isn't. And does it mean anything. Is it important in any way. No, of course it doesn't mean anything. And now the man in the black suit has gone almost all the way over to my parents. And I see him stop. He stands there and looks at them. I sit on the round stone and look at the man in the black suit. What's happening. Where am I actually, yes I'm in the forest but then again this isn't like how things are in a forest, is it. What's happening. And then my mother looks straight at me and she says: so there you are – and I look straight at her and I say: yes, here I am – and it's silent and my mother looks at my father and she says I'm there, there on that stone, I'm sitting on a stone, on that stone there, she says and she points at me, or maybe it's the stone she's pointing at, and she asks my father can't he see, and he answers yes, he sees me, he sees me sitting on a stone, he says, and again there's silence and then my mother looks at me and she says why am I just sitting there, and why don't I answer her when she's talking to me, that's what a person is supposed to do, when someone is talking to them they should answer, she says. I say: I'm answering. And my mother says: yes, you finally answered – and again it's silent, and I see the man in the black suit walk over to my mother and he takes her free hand, and so my mother is standing there holding the man in the black suit with one hand and my father with the other hand, and now I see it, yes, that both my mother and father are standing barefoot in the snow there, they're barefoot too, and are they starting to slowly walk towards me or not, yes, they are, slowly, taking short steps, they come walking towards me, and it's the man in the black suit who's leading them towards me and there, yes, now I see that the radiant presence is there too, but now it's sort of nowhere, it's just around them sort of, yes, it's like a light around them, a light so strong that you almost can't look at it, deep in the dark woods there's a light around my father and mother and around the man in the black suit, a shimmering whiteness is surrounding them, yes, it's like a shape of light is slowly walking towards me and my mother says I have to come now, I can't stay sitting there on that stone, she says, and I think what does she mean by that, that I have to come now, should I stand up, I think, and then I hear my mother say again that I can't just sit there on that stone, I have to get up and come now, she says, and I get up and I take a couple of short steps forwards, and I look down, and I see that now I too am barefoot, and that's strange, because I can't remember taking my shoes off, but I'm barefoot now, that's for sure. And I stand there looking down at my feet, bare in the snow, no, I don't understand this, I think, because I obviously didn't take my shoes off, as cold as it is, but there's so much I don't understand, for example why am I in this forest. Why did I walk away from my car and into this forest, no, it doesn't make sense, not this either and I hear my mother again say I need to come now, I can't stay standing there next to that stone, I mustn't, she says and I take another step forwards and then another and then the man in the black suit reaches out his hand, he holds his hand out to me and I look at him, but I can't see any face, it's like he doesn't have a face, just an empty space where the face should be, and I take his outstretched hand, and then I notice that I'm inside the shimmering white light that now mostly feels like a shining fog, but soft in a way, and nothing is clear, well, it's like I'm in a kind of clarity, in a way, and then the man in the black suit starts slowly walking, and it's like he's walking out of the forest, but to where, I can't say, but I can't see any more trees, or any snow, and that's strange, I think, and I look up, and neither the moon, which was so big and round and yellow, nor the stars are visible, it's a little like we're walking in thin air, yes, this is strange, and the man in the black suit's hand feels neither hot nor cold, and it's like my parents are both there and not there, and it's like we're walking in thin air, yes, yes, we really are walking in thin air, and it's not like we're walking either, but we are moving, yes, well, in a way that's what we're doing, and it's a little like I'm not myself but like I've become part of the shimmering apparition, which now is somehow no longer radiant in its whiteness but, yes, and it sort of doesn't seem like an apparition any more, it's just there, yes, it sort of just is, and words like radiant, like whiteness, like shining, are sort of without any meaning, yes it's like everything is without meaning, and like meanings, yes, meanings don't exist any more, because everything just sort of is, everything is meaning, and we're sort of not walking any more either, yes, we've sort of completely stopped moving, we're in motion without being in motion, and I sort of don't see anything any more either, it's like I'm in a greyness that's holding me, yes, embracing everything that exists, but it's like nothing exists, yes, it's as if everything just is in its greyness, nothing exists and then suddenly I'm inside a light so strong that it's not a light and, no, it can't be any light, it's an emptiness, a void, and yes if it isn't the radiant presence there in front of us, yes, the presence shining in its shimmering whiteness, and it says follow me, and so we follow it, slowly, step by step, breath by breath, the man in the black suit, without a face, my mother, my father, and I, we walk barefoot out into the void, breath by breath, and suddenly there's not a single breath left but only the radiant, shimmering presence that lights up a breathing void, what we're breathing now, with its whiteness.

This translation has been published with the financial
support of NORLA, Norwegian Literature Abroad.